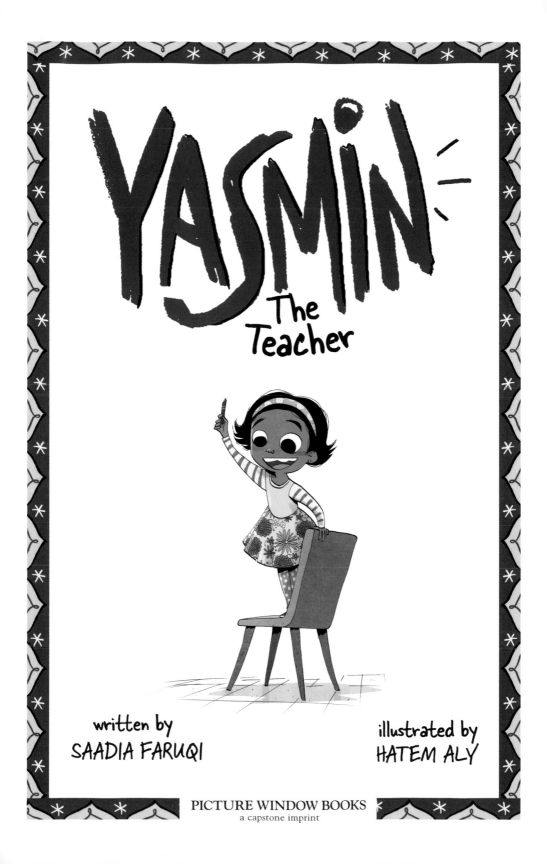

YASMIN
The Teacher

written by
SAADIA FARUQI

illustrated by
HATEM ALY

PICTURE WINDOW BOOKS
a capstone imprint

To Mariam for inspiring me, and Mubashir
for helping me find the right words—S.F.

To my sister, Eman, and her amazing girls,
Jana and Kenzi—H.A.

Yasmin is published by Picture Window Books, a Capstone imprint
1710 Roe Crest Drive
North Mankato, Minnesota 56003
www.mycapstone.com

Library of Congress Cataloging-in-Publication Data
Names: Faruqi, Saadia, author. | Aly, Hatem, illustrator.
Title: Yasmin the teacher / by Saadia Faruqi ; illustrated by Hatem Aly.
Description: North Mankato, Minnesota : Picture Window Books,
[2019] | Series: Yasmin | Summary: When their teacher is called away
from the room she leaves Yasmin in charge, but the other children just
ignore her and start acting silly and noisy—until Yasmin thinks up a
way to motivate them to finish the math assignment, quietly.
Identifiers: LCCN 2018046796| ISBN 9781515837824 (hardcover) |
ISBN 9781515845805 (paperback) | ISBN 9781515837879 (eBook PDF)
Subjects: LCSH: Muslim girls—Juvenile fiction. | Pakistani
Americans—Juvenile fiction. | Elementary schools—Juvenile fiction. |
Responsibility—Juvenile fiction. | CYAC: Pakistani Americans—
Fiction. | Muslims—United States—Fiction. | Schools—Fiction. |
Responsibility—Fiction.
Classification: LCC PZ7.1.F373 Yl 2019 | DDC [E]—dc23
LC record available at https://lccn.loc.gov/2018046796

Editor: Kristen Mohn
Designer: Lori Bye

Design Elements:
Shutterstock: Art and Fashion, rangsan paidaen

Printed in the United States of America.
PA49

TABLE OF CONTENTS

CHAPTER 1

A Present

Yasmin's Aunt Zara came over to Yasmin's house for tea.

"I have a present for you, jaan!" Aunt Zara said. She handed Yasmin a package.

Yasmin ripped it open.

A box of colored pencils!

"I love to color!" Yasmin said.

Then Yasmin noticed a delicious smell. She held the pencils up to her nose. They were scented! Vanilla, strawberry, mango, chocolate!

"Shukriya! Thank you so much!" Yasmin cried. "Please come again with more presents!"

Aunt Zara laughed.

The next day at school,

Yasmin showed her present to

Emma and Ali. "Smell my new

pencils," she said.

Ali took a big sniff.

"Awesome! I wish I had some."

Yasmin was about to say that
Emma and Ali could both choose
a pencil to keep. But then the
bell rang.

CHAPTER 2

Yasmin in Charge

In math class Ms. Alex handed out worksheets. "Work quietly, please," she said.

The problems were difficult, but Yasmin could do them. Counting. Addition. Subtraction.

A knock on the door surprised the students. It was Mr. Nguyen, the principal. "Ms. Alex, can I see you for a minute, please?"

Ms. Alex said, "I'm leaving Yasmin in charge. You all must stay as quiet as little mice. And please finish your worksheets!"

She stepped into the hall and closed the door.

Yasmin couldn't believe she was in charge. She wanted to make Ms. Alex proud.

"Hey, everybody!" yelled Ali.

"Watch my cool moves!"

Ali started dancing on the reading mat. The other students giggled.

Emma began to color on her notepad. "I'm going to draw Yasmin the teacher!" she said loudly.

"Shh!" hissed Yasmin. "We have to be quiet as little mice."

But everyone just talked and laughed. And nobody did their worksheets.

The class was out
of control!

CHAPTER 3

The Scented-Pencil Solution

Yasmin felt like crying.

What could she do to make

Ms. Alex proud?

"Please do your

worksheets!" Yasmin said.

Nobody listened.

Emma was almost done with her picture. "I need pink," she said. "Does anyone have pink?"

That gave Yasmin an idea. The scented pencils! She had plenty to share. She got out her box and waved it in the air.

"How about a competition?" she shouted.

Everyone stopped and looked at her.

"I'll give a scented pencil as a prize to whoever completes the worksheet!" she said.

The students were suddenly quiet as little mice. They sat back down and worked hard at counting, addition, and subtraction.

Ali raised his hand. He needed help. Yasmin showed him how to answer the problem.

"I win!" Ali said as he finished the worksheet.

"Good job!" Yasmin said. "Which pencil would you like?"

Ali chose chocolate. "Thanks, Yasmin!"

Next was Emma. "I'll take strawberry," she said. "Thank you, Yasmin!"

Soon all the students had finished and were quietly drawing with their new pencils.

Ms. Alex returned. "Such well-behaved children!" she said. "Yasmin, you've been an excellent teacher today!"

Yasmin grinned. "Thanks, but I'm glad to be a student again!"

Think About It, Talk About It

* Yasmin feels frustrated when her classmates won't listen to her. Think about a time you felt frustrated. What did you do about it?

* Yasmin has to think creatively to convince her classmates to do their work. If Yasmin didn't have the colored pencils, can you think of other possible solutions for her problem?

* It takes courage to be a leader or to try something new. What are some ways that you give yourself courage when you need it?

Learn Urdu with Yasmin!

Yasmin's family speaks both English and Urdu. Urdu is a language from Pakistan. Maybe you already know some Urdu words!

baba (BAH-bah)—father

bandar (BAHN-dar)—monkey

hijab (HEE-jahb)—scarf covering the hair

jaan (jahn)—life; a sweet nickname for a loved one

mama (MAH-mah)—mother

naan (nahn)—flatbread baked in the oven

nana (NAH-nah)—grandfather on mother's side

nani (NAH-nee)—grandmother on mother's side

salaam (sah-LAHM)—hello

shukriya (shuh-KREE-yuh)—thank you

Pakistan Fun Facts

Yasmin and her family are proud of their Pakistani culture. Yasmin loves to share facts about Pakistan!

Location

Pakistan is on the continent of Asia, with India on one side and Afghanistan on the other.

Islamabad

PAKISTAN

Education

There are 51 universities and 155,000 primary schools in Pakistan.

First Female Leader

Benazir Bhutto became the first female Prime Minister of Pakistan, and of any Muslim nation.

Sports

The official sport of Pakistan is field hockey.

Make Scented Pencils!

SUPPLIES:

- wooden pencils
- newspaper
- scissors
- tape
- water
- fruit juices such as lemon, lime, or orange
- one large bowl (big enough to hold pencils) for each type of juice
- plate

STEPS:

1. Cut out pieces of newspaper wide enough to fit the length of the pencil and long enough to wrap around a few times. Wrap each pencil tightly and use tape to keep the paper in place.

2. Pour water into one bowl and mix in one kind of juice. Add enough juice to make a strong scent. Then fill the other bowls with water and one kind of juice in each.

3. Put one or more paper-covered pencils into each bowl. Let soak for 1 to 3 hours.

4. Take the pencils out and place them on a plate in a sunny spot. Let sit for 1 to 3 hours.

5. Once the pencils are dry, remove the newspaper. Now your pencils will have cool scents!

Saadia Faruqi is a Pakistani American
writer, interfaith activist, and cultural
sensitivity trainer previously profiled
in *O Magazine*. She is author of the
adult short story collection, *Brick Walls:
Tales of Hope & Courage from Pakistan*.
Her essays have been published in
Huffington Post, *Upworthy*, and *NBC
Asian America*. She resides in Houston,
Texas, with her husband and children.

Hatem Aly is an Egyptian-born illustrator whose work has been featured in multiple publications worldwide. He currently lives in beautiful New Brunswick, Canada, with his wife, son, and more pets than people. When he is not dipping cookies in a cup of tea or staring at blank pieces of paper, he is usually drawing books. One of the books he illustrated is *The Inquisitor's Tale* by Adam Gidwitz, which won a Newbery Honor and other awards, despite Hatem's drawings of a farting dragon, a two-headed cat, and stinky cheese.

Join Yasmin on all her adventures!

Discover more at